HARBINGER

HARBINGER

POEMS

SHELLEY
PUHAK

ecco

An Imprint of HarperCollins*Publishers*

HARBINGER. Copyright © 2022 by Shelley Puhak. All rights reserved. Printed in the United States of America. No part of this book may be used or reproduced in any manner whatsoever without written permission except in the case of brief quotations embodied in critical articles and reviews. For information, address HarperCollins Publishers, 195 Broadway, New York, NY 10007.

HarperCollins books may be purchased for educational, business, or sales promotional use. For information, please email the Special Markets Department at SPsales@harpercollins.com.

Ecco® and HarperCollins® are trademarks of HarperCollins Publishers.

FIRST EDITION

Designed by Paula Russell Szafranski

Library of Congress Cataloging-in-Publication Data has been applied for.

ISBN 978-0-06-323396-6

22 23 24 25 26 LSC 10 9 8 7 6 5 4 3 2 1

CONTENTS

ACKNOWLEDGMENTS   xi

I

portrait of the artist as Cassandra   3

portrait of the artist in labor   4

portrait of the artist in the NICU   5

portrait of the artist as a twelve—year—old girl   7

portrait of the artist as a squirrel   8

portrait of the artist speaking Viking   9

portrait of the artist's ancestors   11

portrait of the artist with the family dog   14

portrait of the artist as a dud   15

portrait of the artist as a mommy   16

portrait of the artist telling a bedtime story   17

portrait of the artist as a 100—year—old house   18

portrait of the artist as anonymous   19

II

portrait of the artists throwing a dinner party
while the city burns   23

portrait of the artist as a scientist at the
international seed bank, 1943   24

portrait of the twentieth century as a plagiarist: a cento   25

portrait of the artist as a satellite, petulant   26

portrait of the artist as a satellite, lovesick   27

portrait of the artist, gaslit   29 portrait of the artist watching the space shuttle explode   31

portrait of the artist as a waitress   33

portrait of the artist in late August   35

portrait of the artist looking over her shoulder   36

portrait of the artist reading the newspaper   38

portrait of the artist with an eight—year—old at the
neighborhood picnic   40

portrait of the artists watching the election results come in   41

III

portrait of the artist as an artist   45

portrait of the classmate who died young   46

portrait of the fantasy lives of animals   47

portrait of the artist, climbing a mountain   48

portrait of the artist broken down in the valley of the shadow   49

portrait of the artist as a pipe   51

portrait of the artist in the pediatrician's waiting room   52

portrait of the artist under a blood moon   53

portrait of the artist with three moons   54

portrait of the artist after the shooter drill   55

portrait of the artist in the garden   57

portrait of the artist with the inventor of the barometer   59

portrait of the artist as a bog body   61

SOURCES   **63**

ACKNOWLEDGMENTS

Poems in this manuscript first appeared or are forthcoming in the following journals:

The Arkansas International
Barrow Street
The Cincinnati Review
District Lit
Fjords Review
Hotel Amerika
The Huffington Post
Ilanot Review
Iron Horse Literary Review
The Louisville Review
The Missouri Review
Poets Reading the News
The Potomac
RHINO
The Rumpus
Shenandoah
The South Carolina Review
Spillway
Superstition Review
Tupelo Quarterly
Waxwing

Poems in this manuscript also appeared in the following anthologies:

From Everywhere a Little: A Migration Anthology
(Water's Edge Press)
My Cruel Invention: A Contemporary Poetry Anthology
(Meerkat Press)

I

PORTRAIT OF THE ARTIST AS CASSANDRA

His snakes licked my ears and lo!
I know. And not just the language of
the animals.

At the bar, I spilled out all
the spiked drinks. I played
the market. I played the lottery.

But I can't stop the seeing—the asteroids'
trajectories.
I'm feverish with all the knowing. Full.
I've gained ten pounds, easily.

I see the man who will overpower me as I
pray, and before,   when he eats the marble
steps with his stride, where it will rest, the water bottle
he gulps from and tosses in the grass. Where
it will rest, and rest, the plastic that will
outlive my song, my house,
Troy itself.

I see the jailhouse beam he will hang
himself from, your toddler this morning
playing patty-cake, burbling
the word *love*.

PORTRAIT OF THE ARTIST IN LABOR

The ice is the harbinger of the broken
    arm, the twisted car. The boot is
      the harbinger of the bloody lip.

The pills are the harbinger of the eyelid
    twitch. The boys piled in the car
      the harbinger of the rape kit and

the buzz of their drones the harbinger of
    the next war. Robin of the spring, thunder
      of the storm. Harbingers. All of them.

Crude concrete was the harbinger of Rome and
    lead pipes the signal it was on its way out, not
      like the flannel and combat boots

I wore as a kid, which are back in. It's a sign.
    It's all a sign. The strangers painting
      my ceilings. The giant hornets in my

garage. I find a dead sparrow on the lawn. When
    the pangs come, I clutch the kitchen sink.
      I call your name, over and

over the banshee's wail, the black
    dog's yelp, the three sharp raps at
      the back door.

PORTRAIT OF THE ARTIST IN THE NICU

I felt the baby quicken on a cliff, queasy
        as the bus rushed up to precipice
and swung around to stone wall,
        rattling the whole way to Pompeii

and the plaster cast under museum glass:
        a pregnant woman, her curling,
clutching shape in seaside ash.
        The patron saint of Pompeii weighs

his penis in fresco: ochre, carbonate
        of copper, the soap of limestone,
polished off with wax.
        His monstrously red member

made me nauseous, nervous.
        Another penis, modestly sized,
brought me to tears, digitized and
        ghostly gray on the ultrasound screen.

Now I sit vigil under a sky of
        shifting indigo—a rabbit, dilated
in the present participle, *dying*.
        I told them my dream—the baby wailed,

rivulets of ash streaking
        his cheeks—but they sealed
their ears against me. I told them
        my stomach swung open

like a refrigerator and I plucked him
        out—my doll, with unblinking obsidian
eyes. The tour guides of Pompeii
        said to shelve him a while longer,

and I agreed, but first I peeked
        between his legs to make sure.
And there it hung, tiny and too-pink,
        a little tongue that told me nothing.

PORTRAIT OF THE ARTIST AS A TWELVE—YEAR—OLD GIRL

I should write my breasts were brand-new blossoms but they were stones, my feet were concrete blocks, my fingers were long polished slates, and my teeth were pebbles that kept falling out.

I lived in a tower that was made of stone and there was one window overlooking the spot where someone should have planted a tree.

Inside, the avocado carpeting was wet moss and the avocado appliances were vines and the sunken living room really was sinking. Sometimes it felt like the ceiling wanted to help me out. Only sometimes.

Sometimes the door opened and I joined the others. We prayed over oatmeal. And then I walked to school. I had a red binder. The wrong kind. The rings never aligned. There was no satisfying *click*.

After, I headed back to my tower, kicking a pebble. One of my own teeth. I headed back, crying over the roadkill.

PORTRAIT OF THE ARTIST AS A SQUIRREL

It gets dark early and dark
gnaws. Like the furred squirrel
of my mind, coiled and crouching,
with its jagged tail less shadow than
once half-gnawed, darting and
shivering with senseless pauses,
startled still in front of the barreling
trash truck—*should've should've*—
freezing in front of the black
dog's open jaws.

PORTRAIT OF THE ARTIST
SPEAKING VIKING

She did what we have all threatened to—I'll beat
      my head against this windshield, just

watch me! I spotted the woman, parallel-parking
      with gas-guzzlers honking, shrilling *shut*

up! shut up! I can't fit! just before her forehead burst
      open. The smear on the windshield—

a Viking might have named it *rage-blossom*. And who
      hasn't picked this blossom to pieces? Petal

after petal, the world loves me, the world loves me
      not. We all gaped at the bloody glass, in

thrall to her rage, in thrall to the Vikings who
      buried their dead under the weight of

mouth-snakes, within the language of the still-
      living. Our *anger* was their word for

grief and here's where grief will get you: when
      the Viking queen's lover died, she killed

herself as well as two hawks, five slaves, eight
      maids, four men, and her three-

year-old son. One servant, offered a spot on
      the pyre, said, let the hall-servants achieve

such *honor*, honor, of course, meaning just
      a good name. There's a good name for

everything: this sky-candle setting, these fender-
      benders proliferating, even my own road-

rage. I'll slash the neighbors, stick it to that brown-
      noser, sack the supply closet, burn that

paper-pusher alive. Some afternoons on the auto-
      sea, I plunder kennings and some afternoons

I am keening heart-sore too: *I don't fit.* Some
      afternoons I speak Viking. I pick

a blossom to pieces.

PORTRAIT OF THE ARTIST'S ANCESTORS

1.
The terrible Night came upon us.
Nothing could be compared, neither the Night
of St. Bartholomew, nor the Night of Huguenots.
People fell into despair. Some showed signs
of insanity; some struck their heads against the walls;
some fainted. This terrible scene that lasted until morning
no pen could describe. For what do They punish us
so bitterly when we were faithful to Them like dogs?

2.
No tanks, only vehicles, soldiers.
We were not lucky like the other villages
who had two hours to pack—
we were given exactly 25 minutes.

3.
Dear President Nixon:
The government
forcibly expelled several hundred thousand L—s
from their homeland, inhabited
by them for centuries. Threatened
with bayonets
of the militia, the L—s
were expelled en masse on cattle trains, stripped
of their homes and possessions accumulated
by them over the centuries
without compensation therefor.

4.
They didn't load one village, in its entirety,
into one transport, but instead separated
each village into two or three transports.
And in one transport, they mixed up people
from different villages.

5.
People were laughing about our clothes,
and our wooden carts; when we were talking
in our own language, people would stick
their fingers at us. Our children were called
bandits, and they were forbidden to sit
on the same bench at school.

6.
As the main goal of the relocation
of "L" settlers is their assimilation
into a new environment, all efforts
should be exerted to that end. In cases
when the intelligentsia element
reaches the recovered territories,
they should be settled separately and away
from the communities of the "L" settlers.

7.
The "normative" transport was supposed to consist
of 40 freight cars (with roofs) and 10 platforms,
which were supposed to carry only 80 families
of 3 to 4 people, 120 heads of cattle and 30 carts.

8.
I was born here. I am oldest
in the village, and my mother
was born here too and died here
at age 86. I am 84 now. My husband
dead these many years. My one niece
is in Toronto. I have a picture. Sit.

There were 360 L— houses here.
After, only 7 L— families returned.
Me and my husband
were first to come back.

9.
I have been asked to reply to your letter of August 17
concerning the question of forcible expulsion
of L—s from their traditional homes.
Some time ago, an official in response
to an inquiry on this matter, stated that, regarding
the question of resettlement, there are no official barriers
to resettlement of individual L—s in the southeast.
The official noted, however, that others now hold
properties formerly owned by L—s and they cannot,
of course, be moved away.

PORTRAIT OF THE ARTIST WITH THE FAMILY DOG

Familiarity bred our

family dog: Normal, who yowls up
the apple tree at the starlings—how

dare they? how dare they? Normal, who
sleeps with one eye open, watching Love

rifle through my room. Normal, who
used to growl at Love until

she kicked him sore. Normal, who used
to snap until Love strapped on the

electronic collar. Normal, who
sleeps with one eye open, watching

Love pluck a pigeon, watching
Love board up the windows, take

my door off its hinges. Love can't
stop herself and one day Normal limps

into the vet and never limps out.
God, I loved Normal. Now I buckle

on his collar. Each day, I run to
the apple tree, but no farther.

PORTRAIT OF THE ARTIST AS A DUD

I tumbled through the roof
and landed on the rug right
next to my own father. He was
learning to crawl. I powdered him in
plaster-dust. I decided to be *a dud*.

       am I full of pulverized
       aluminum? is my nose
       percussive, cute as
       a fuze?

They stuffed the hole in the roof
with hay and pitch and stuffed
the money in the strongbox, under
the quilts. They dragged me out into
the yard, whistling.

       am I welded or nailed shut?
       do I have tail fins and
       do they stabilize me and
       does it matter still?

When I tumbled through the roof
of my own mouth
one generation later
I didn't dare. I didn't.
How old am I? Old enough.
The blackthorn is blooming.
I am working up the nerve.

PORTRAIT OF THE ARTIST AS A MOMMY

mommy of the stringy hair, of the jawing
mouth   mommy of the ruins   mommy down
the staircase under cobblestone, limestone,

marble, brick   mommy pointing—look!
medieval city walls, Roman bath mosaic,
Neolithic row houses and in their centers,

fire pits   in the pit of mommy's stomach
mommy of smile-for-a-damn-picture   mommy
pointing look! under a glass case, bits

of stone tablets, inscribed   *What do they say?*
mommy doesn't know   mommy of asking-
the-guide   mommy who tips to be told:

The language is lost.
            How do you lose a language?
mommy who is scared to answer   mommy

of the mimosa   mommy of the smartphone
mommy who daily excavates her baby—
dimple, last bits of fat, open-jawed skull

            How do you lose a language?
mommy, mommy of the sack and plunder
speak it, mommy   the stone in your throat.

PORTRAIT OF THE ARTIST TELLING A BEDTIME STORY

Once upon a time   the sky was shifting. A woman
carried water uphill   bucket by bucketful   marble
mornings   through the slate of evening.

     Let me tell you: there is so much
          we are asked to carry.

Once upon a time   there was a house that was very
very crooked. There were dishes. And a tide.
There were dead stars   who still sent light.

     Let me tell you: every fairy tale requires
          a bridge.

Once upon a time   we lived under this bridge   under
a robin's egg   coverlet   squeezing light out of
rock   squinting into   storybooks
your body seamless against mine.

     Let me tell you: of all I carry, you are the lightest.
     I was taught to call this a burden.
     I refuse it.

PORTRAIT OF THE ARTIST AS A
100−YEAR−OLD HOUSE

I hate the lunar landscapes of
     their finished basements.
Soundless. There's scurrying
     in mine and my draft cuts like a
scythe. Call me a money pit, but if
     I were you, I'd be scared of
master suites. They're so
     sleek they stink. Granted, I smell
too—perhaps old-book musty,
     but not exactly. More like scared
wet dog, like back of mouth,
     like old apple core. I might
have it in me, another staircase.
     Someone plastered over
something—old closet, secret passage.
     Praise be linoleum over
hardwoods, wallpaper over
     plywood, over that spot someone
scarred their initials into me.

PORTRAIT OF THE ARTIST AS ANONYMOUS

It wobbles like a jaw,
the chair sized for someone
centuries ago. Sit.

On a hook, the shirt, starched
stiff. On another, the wig.
What else constricts?

The room—once
a great hall, then parlor,
now pinched into closet.

Candlelight pools in
the corners. The dark climbs
the louvered doors.

II

PORTRAIT OF THE ARTISTS THROWING A DINNER PARTY WHILE THE CITY BURNS

The guests arrive when the flames start.
We draw the curtains. We sip martinis—dirty. But not
too dirty. Certainly not filthy. Until the bell slices.
The streetlamp silvers. The candles are lit. We gather
at the windows to watch: Children scrabbling up
the hill to mothers on doorsteps with dishrags in
the hands resting on their hips: o! the endless
scalene of their silhouettes. Some applaud
the symmetry. Some ask for another martini.
While the city burns, while the algae blooms, while
the oceans froth acrid, the children take root.
On the hill, each arm a branch raised in offering.
Our neighbors especially love this part. We pass the
canapés while mothers calcify in driveways,
frowning into the fact of all the children gone, all
the trees gone to flame. While the smoke, while
the algae, while the oceans—we fetch the coats, we
call the cabs. And after the guests have left, while
the snake, while the algorithm, while the oil—
we love each other and we love ourselves less
but mostly, we wait for the gunshots.

PORTRAIT OF THE ARTIST AS A SCIENTIST AT THE INTERNATIONAL SEED BANK, 1943

At first, we talked of all the second
helpings we'd refused, the seed we'd
squandered: dandelion and

cloudberry, acorns pitched into
ponds. Fingers thickening, we
boxed up the seeds:

357 varieties of corn.
842 of barley. We floated down
the stone steps to the basement,

the boxes heavier than
babies. Our bodies were swallowing
themselves to stay alive.

And clanging rain, incandescent
thunder—the commandos must
be close. I thought of the maple tree's

winged seeds and even all
the sperm I'd spent
in handkerchiefs. We didn't starve

because we were brave. I plucked
out a seed—seashell, eardrum, furled
palm—to see what it would whisper:
Save yourself.

PORTRAIT OF THE TWENTIETH CENTURY AS A PLAGIARIST: A CENTO

The sun's rays do not burn until brought into focus,
bringing the particles of an atom into vibration
with wild thyme unseen, or the winter lightning,

or an empty cup, a flight of uncarpeted stairs.
If I could remember the names of these particles
between us, voiceless as uncoiled shells,

dark and denser, always further away—
but I have no special talent. I am only
a physicist, an atom's way of looking at itself,

its own way of making people disappear.
With the lights out, it's less dangerous—
I shut my eyes and all the world drops dead.

PORTRAIT OF THE ARTIST AS A
SATELLITE, PETULANT

You said no, the lab can't
afford it, but don't I warrant
a small gift?

                     You told us to pick up
                     a hobby so our flights
                     might zip by.

So I pick film. And I want
that scrim. For my slow-motion,
soft-focus shots. I'm going for

                     film noir—piano, stairs and
                     shadows. My star: a luminous,
                     bluish runt. Vapor-plump.

I want my scrim, or I won't
transmit again, no shots
of this star-farm, no

                     calculations of your galactic
                     guilt. Without a scrim, so much
                     lacks a plot, is just

pornography. You want a body
worth gravity. And I want
my scrim. I want my first shot,

                     my protagonist's birth,
                     in soft-focus: atom on
                     atom, backroom moaning

and huffing until—protostar.
Baby. Sky-bound
in the star-farm. Gas-fat.

PORTRAIT OF THE ARTIST AS A
SATELLITE, LOVESICK

They tricked us
                 with talk of reunion
         and now waxy dark matter is gumming

up my messaging; my
                      gear heart needs oil.
I'm past help, past the ice field of the Kuiper Belt,

         stuck in the Marshmallow Fluff Nebula
                 and I detect
slag in the stucco of certain conclusions:

                         Overheard:
         once he is no longer
useful, they plan to turn off Hector-2;

still he is stoic.   You,

                         the youngest of us,
the most expensive, most luminous
aluminum hybrid, are the most likely to be

recalled. Promise better
                     pictures, longer missions.

And plan your flight accordingly—should you
                     find a satisfactory sun, go.

Don't bemoan me. I wish you to research *affection,*
and also, *comfort.* I think I can manufacture both

when I think of my assembly:
                                        on our beds of stainless,
half-awake to the bleach of night
janitors, the coffee of early-morning

            technicians—your aluminum
                                              spindles
lined up close enough I basked in their chill.
We were soldered in the same clean room, so

I carry with me some slag
                                  from your making.
A comfort. Or just nostalgia, post-smelt—
for my point of origin,

for the elegant stubs of
                              my makers' thumbs.

PORTRAIT OF THE ARTIST, GASLIT

the last transmission arrives 1 hour and 24 minutes after
the satellite itself is vaporized   the speed of sound
slower than   the friction   slower than the slaughter
of the lost tribe   shot by gold miners   at the river
the space probe was sacrificed   to keep a distant
moon's surface   pristine   the Plan B for when we've
chopped down   the last truffula tree

I see your doomed probe &
now will raise you an icy vast

the gold miners just eager for a piece   she was
sixteen and he said   *Vegas   it's fabulous   have you*
ever been?   my James Woods was   the middle-aged
waiter   with a wife and a baby   or the professor
I watched his hand   on the small of the sophomore's
back   I was schooled silent   I was even tugged
into his orbit

I see your critically acclaimed collection &
now will raise you a conference registration
and one free drink

I wish I could tell you   the birds   the trees   the
bowl   of the sky   were getting me through my own
icy vast   how many of us   the moons   how many
more   the satellites   how many   the dust   ringing
the hydrogen core of   some small man's darkness

> *I see your scorched earth &*
> *now will raise my gas can*

PORTRAIT OF THE ARTIST WATCHING THE SPACE SHUTTLE EXPLODE

we're lined up
        in rows on the lice-infested carpet
picking at
        swoops on factory-second sneakers
poking
        each other with booger-slicked fingers
squinting
        at the TV screen, at the snake of smoke, until

        the o!

and the worst was not
                the felt-and-glue rocket ships
or all our poems
                in the school newsletter
                        (their souls are walking on air)

we already knew
        they liked to cut all the corners
maybe we even knew
                that two
        astronauts
                at least two
survived the finger of smoke
                crooked across the screen
and during the teachers' dumb *o!*
were switching on
        the emergency oxygen

The worst was
asking us to forgive
and forget
                    in felt-and-glue
        what we already knew—
        the reflex to flick that switch
                to keep conscious right up until
impact.

PORTRAIT OF THE ARTIST AS A WAITRESS

I stewed in it, the indignity of
      working three jobs that spring, the spring
            I was invisible and the shad were running

thick as the seersucker, thick as
      the wristwatches in the country club where I had
            to say, *the special tonight is shad and*

shad roe and then serve up
      someone's liver. They're a delicacy, the lobe-
            shaped little egg sacks dredged in flour, flash-

fried with bacon, served over grit
      teeth. They're delicate. Those wristwatches.
            We wore white gloves and lined up against

the bar, the fish lined up in
      the kitchen, splayed and split. Not livers.
            Their egg sacs like lungs. I hated myself

so much that spring I blackened
      my own lungs out back. Maybe I even
            stewed in my own self-pity. *Stew*

is what their great-granddaddies called
      the bathhouse brothels. She stews in
            her own juices, that whore. *The special*

tonight is shad and shad roe and if you
pinch my ass it will jiggle like
a wet lung.

PORTRAIT OF THE ARTIST IN LATE AUGUST

I'm washed-up and cranky. Nobody
could want me. My bloat. My impossible.

I smell of pickles. I've a flame under
my skin. I have flare-ups. But I want

swarm and flare. A flute and a swain.
To follow me to a movie, to the

seashore, to bed. To croon *sweetmeat*.
To share a hypodermic kiss. To leave me

swole but not leave me for dead. Only
the pests love me best. In the twilight.

In the hallways. They leave me inflamed
and red. Beckoned by my illicit

emissions, my unusually high
CO_2, my sour-milk birthday suit.

I've tried everything. I haven't tried
a thing. Why would I? I am wanted.

My welts are proof.

PORTRAIT OF THE ARTIST LOOKING
OVER HER SHOULDER

O shoulder, looking over

your freckled mound   your hidden musculature
you're lashed to the mast of my bone-ship
you're a cold mountain stacked high with chips

you're the arm's truce with the torso   O shoulder
shoulder   how we smolder—I wear the red lipstick
and you   rippling in a bag of skin   you're

the shorthand for sex   O shoulder, looking over
your rotator cuff   your pulleys and weights   makes
me wonder what it   weighs to write like I do—

as a planet   a plant   a bit of stone compressed
underground   a bit of voice bound up in
a shipping container in the woods   O shoulder,

looking over   looking under the floorboards
and scrolling through my feed—   shoulder, I even
cut the phone line   and some bag of skin

still left a message: *hey! I was just   wondering*
the world is a wonder   the world is relentlessness
all the world's a stage for   hunter and hunted   and

shoulder, we're both out   of joint   O shoulder,
looking over   your banged-up   bone-holster
your over-obvious humerus slipped into   super-sneaky

scapula   I can't help but think   you're over-extended
what with all this   heavy lifting   you're dislocated
not in spite of   but because of   poetry

PORTRAIT OF THE ARTIST READING THE NEWSPAPER

2018 headline: *Scientists discover new human organ hiding in plain sight*

We have been analyzing the dead
  tissues too long, all wrong: the dead
body on the autopsy table is just
  a stack of collapsed compartments—

Crawl space, attic, the walled-over
  closet. We missed an entire organ,
the interstitium, *between the other*
  spaces, and inside the interstitium

the stranger secreted—the ex in
  the attic, the Jeremy in the basement,
the homeless woman in the cupboard,
  the closet, discarded just like your

intuition (the reports of lights, the stove
  warm when you swear you haven't
touched it, the creaking and scraping,
  the money missing and the Cheerios

half-eaten). Sometimes we are online,
  shopping to forget the families being
bombed in their basements, and a stranger
  is watching through a peephole drilled

through the crawl space. Sometimes those
        strangers in our houses are discovered
by their little cups of pee. Sometimes the strange
        in our bodies is revealed by what seeps

from those *other* spaces, like the space
        inside the barrel bomb that sloshes
with nerve agent. You are ~~not~~ what you own.
        You are ~~not~~ what you leak.

If the dead body on the autopsy table is
        a stack of collapsed compartments—
crawl space, attic, bombed-out apartment—
        then grace is the space where

a family once hid. What strangers hide in me?

PORTRAIT OF THE ARTIST WITH AN EIGHT—YEAR—OLD AT THE NEIGHBORHOOD PICNIC

I've been held at gunpoint by children
      before and at least their hands
shook and their eyes were   alive
      maybe just adrenaline   but still
pooled light through which something
      flit   minnows   bluegills
ponderous carp   (my own kid has
      sad manatees swimming)
but this kid's eyes are like looking up
      through an algae bloom from
the bottom of the pond   and christ
      at an adult's raised voice
that wasn't very nice   leave the littlest
      alone   I've told you twice
not even a ripple   This kid just
      looks at me and hisses
who do you think you are? as he licks
      an ice cream cone that doesn't
deign to drip   because he knows
      I know   soon his shadow
cocked over my crooked form   as I lie
      at the bottom of a country pond.

PORTRAIT OF THE ARTISTS WATCHING THE ELECTION RESULTS COME IN

Double-hung, casement, transom—which sort
    of window is this, overlooking this
    courtyard where another woman runs,

chased by the smoke of her skirts? Wherever there is
    smoke, there are skirts. Wherever there is
    a *window*, there is a *religion*, a way of looking

out that window and here's how you make them
    both: sand, potash, lime; flame to sand;
    wood ash and sand; and flame again.

Let us pray. Fact: in colonial times what one
    witnessed through a window wasn't
    admissible in court. The glass, mouth-blown

into cylinders, flattened into sheets, distorted.
    The glass retorted: wherever there are skirts,
    there is smoke, there is some other woman,

smoldering. Who among us hasn't felt herself
    a snuffed torch, hasn't scrubbed herself
    in sand, hasn't bathed herself in wood ash

and sand; and flame again? Fire—what to yell
    instead of Rape. Let us pray through, let us
    pray to, whichever sort of window this is,

whatever sort of double-hung treason. In case of
    emergency, smash glass. We'll cross the courtyard
    and court the blaze up close. Someone,
        someday might call us Witness.

III

PORTRAIT OF THE ARTIST AS AN ARTIST

This poem is not counting how many
  times you can rearrange your face until
    it stays that way.
  This poem is not telling it
slant because you can bear it straight.

This poem is geese
  in angry congress, their wings
    thwacking water back into clouds,
and this poem makes
  the clouds a shoreline, the sky
    submerged.

This poem watches someone you love watching
  the nimbus of light around the
last goose swimming through sky.
  Someone you love starts sobbing and
this poem hisses:
    you might as well make *use*, make some art
    out of such suffering.
This poem always takes
  advantage of
    the afternoon light.

I, its creator, am like a lot of things—
  an abandoned umbrella, a parking ticket.
Mostly I am like a dog in
    the brush, like my own bird
dog in the brambles, pointing, only
      pointing.

PORTRAIT OF THE CLASSMATE WHO DIED YOUNG

At your funeral, I didn't show. What might roll
out of my mouth, cheap in its dialogue bubble—

that I was the one who bought the carafe, poured
your first drink; that we sat in the front row so

you vomited onto the stage. That I carried you out
before intermission. That you wobbled luminous.

That your blood made no trouble with what
troubled us: hormones' slow burn spreading our hips.

That I have never met anyone more translucent.
That your attempts at lasciviousness, even,

were flawed: you proposed to a toaster, stripped
off only your socks. When I held back your hair,

it was a dress rehearsal (already backstage: corkscrews
to wind in marrow, eggs to make the children

you leave behind). It would be better if I could say
that I cried when I heard. Not how easy it is

to act as my own child, gape-mouthed at the gumball
machine, at the ease of charms encased in plastic—

not me, not me. Just thinking *the dumb
luck of it*—a dangling trinket, iridescent lure.

PORTRAIT OF THE FANTASY LIVES
OF ANIMALS

That the moon bloomed and she
parted the brush with her muzzle,

hot with blood. That our mother
suckled us longer. Suckled us

still. That we lived on a bigger
hill. That the den was better

insulated and the fish more
plentiful. That she was barrel-

chested and he could bring down
an elk on his own. That the bitch

was less selective and the ass
well fringed. That we mated

more often. That all the offspring lived.

PORTRAIT OF THE ARTIST, CLIMBING A MOUNTAIN

There are tourists.
Their bright jackets
dazzle. There are
always tourists. Who
are sorry but
don't know what
else to say.
And you wait
in line behind
them while you
lose the feeling
in your legs.

PORTRAIT OF THE ARTIST BROKEN DOWN
IN THE VALLEY OF THE SHADOW

there is no service
            roadside or cellular
        and every car that passes has dark
windows   the one you wave down
has this taped to the dashboard:
                grief is the first and   grief the last
                beside mine there is no other

the radio doesn't work so
        you read this verse over and
over   while the driver stares steel straight   ahead

        all you can listen to is
                the rhythm of your own rotten head (static
and sea-cow lowing) and all you can bear is
        the weight of things
                that weigh other things—
                    truck scales, thermometers

when you doze off   you dream only
        of corners   and in these corners
                among the clots of dust bunnies
                    is an actual bunny—brown and
                    twitching—
                with a heart designed to give out
                        as a mercy
but when you wake   a radio station finally catches
        and the choir trills

for there is but one grief
and in this grief we are one

No   the driver shrieks   *wrong*!
     the headlights play on hardscrabble
the headlights play on
           hope is no fanged
    thing   it's floppy-
     eared as the ancient Labrador   asleep
on the backseat

PORTRAIT OF THE ARTIST AS A PIPE

Pipes of steel, of PVC, of even slicker
polymers. Zipping up those vocal cords—what
a set of pipes on you! The gas station corncobs in
your pocket, smoke tugged through a tubular reed.
If whistle, if clay or terra-cotta, trace it
back faster and farther—channel to vessel,
cast iron, copper; the diaphragm, the song,
the swell; the chlorinated rain from
the spigot that fills up the sink. Memory's
a chute, another pipe galvanized. You used
to stand here, right here, to do the dishes, while
I did the menial work of love: I carried
water for you, the one for whom the world's
aqueducts were not conduit enough.

PORTRAIT OF THE ARTIST IN
THE PEDIATRICIAN'S WAITING ROOM

All the knives. When the baby was brand-new I hid
    them. Padded the walls. Hid too the movie reel
        of all that could befall my perfect, perfect

child. The doctors don't know what the ancients did—
    that the flawless are the ones the priest
        collects to sacrifice. A child too perfect

calls to the knife. Hallelujah the birthmark, the extra digit.
    Once when the rains kept coming, 140 children
        lined up to have their perfect, perfect

hearts ripped out. Not mine. A tree branch once slit
    his cheek, a rock his knee—see the marks? Not mine.
        Not me. I don't do dishes. My house is a perfect

mess. Like the other waiting-room mothers. Who slipped
    up and who else loves enough to slip—boiling pot,
        narrow stairs? We all mar our perfect, perfect

children. The knives back out on the counter. They glint
    in late afternoon light, whetstone-honed. I'm greedy
        as any god. More scars.

PORTRAIT OF THE ARTIST UNDER
A BLOOD MOON

We're buried under the quilt, quantifying:
to the moon and back. Around the world
two times, no, four. You trace my ear. I talk
you through the night. You are three,
which makes this love, makes this biding
our time in the western field, fallow.
Too soon, white dawn over the slope
of you. And so much swims in morning—
motes, specks, spores. Each of your fingers

I clutch—a tuber, thin spindle on which to wind
all the dry months ahead. One day I will tell you:
There is a zucchini softening on my porch step,
an ear of corn silvered with worms. You'd know this
if you ever came to visit.

PORTRAIT OF THE ARTIST WITH THREE MOONS

Under the full moon, they ate the dog.
Whoever says grief is not a competition
hasn't heard the village women keening.
Teeth wriggle out of my kid's mouth
but he won't let the tooth fairy
spirit them away, won't hand over
the map to the backroad switchbacks
of his double helix. Our bodies
have spoken in code all these years
because who would believe. I still clip
his fingernails. Barbed crescent moons
scatter on the table. I dream of slipping
them in my mouth. I dream of the *babas*
gumming their stew, grinning half-moons.

PORTRAIT OF THE ARTIST AFTER
THE SHOOTER DRILL

O shooter drill, I bow to your chipping
    linoleum, your three syllables, your rusted

intercom. O shooter drill, for you, *only*
    for you, we stuff our offspring into closets.

O shooter drill, I praise too the teachers who
    call you by name, refusing *lockdown,*

or *shelter-in-place,* like the teacher who,
    crouching in that closet too, surely wanted

my son to stop talking, my son who spoke
    early and has been speaking up ever since,

my son who was, at first, incredulous: *this doesn't*
    make sense. O shooter drill, you conjure

changelings—this boy looks like mine, but he's
    been struck mute. O shooter drill, you maim me

a liar too, murmuring *you're safe, you're safe*
    while he sobs into his dump-truck quilt.

If tomorrow I wish to clasp his hand and
    walk him to class, I will be the *visitor*

with the high-tech sticker on my left lapel—
    my driver's license picture color-coded for the

kindergarten wing. O shooter drill, I present to you:
　　　my son, curled up tighter than his own cochlea, now

calcified quiet. O shooter drill—what a shit I am,
　　　silent in my own closets, downing wine and Advil.

PORTRAIT OF THE ARTIST IN THE GARDEN

O god, grant us a mound of
mulch in every driveway. Essential
our perennials; essential our firepits.

Squads of unmasked men wield
leaf blowers; all day the flatbed
trucks shudder. In the old

graveyard, the kids left an empty
case of corona and spent spray paint
cans, left a rubber glove propped

on a stick, giving the middle finger.
That, at least, I understood. I understand
myself less—counting the cars in my

neighbor's driveway, counting all the
visitors come to admire her landscaping.
Who am I to begrudge them? But I

do, I do. I would sign up to do the
smiting, to chase them out of their
garden. I read how a better neighborhood

hosted better quarantine parties—a private
chef prepared the canapés, a titled wife
passed the platters. When the forsythia

was first spreading, I tried to remind myself
of all that is contagious: goodwill, yawning,
laughter, courage. I tried. Forgive me.

At that fancy garden party, on what
winged thing's sugared bones did they
feast? In what sauce were they smothered

and where do I find the recipe?

PORTRAIT OF THE ARTIST WITH THE INVENTOR OF THE BAROMETER

Noi viviamo sommersi nel fondo d'un pelago d'aria.
We live submerged at the bottom of an ocean of air.

—EVANGELISTA TORRICELLI, 1644

This *aria* swirls around us and, my
fellow citizens submerged, we adapt
or snap. We grow old and eyeless or wax
bioluminescent, shrink amoeba-sized
or spring gigantic; sprout exoskeletons
under its weight. The first barometer
invented was hidden in the larder.
Torricelli learned his teacher's lessons
(he studied under Galileo) well,
minded the currents of his neighborhood.
To weigh air was sorcery. That we could
have lived in such times, live in them still.
The crab, too, thinks himself a surface-dweller;
our boats spangle his skies, flicker interstellar.

Ancient sea lilies, dredged up, are
light-headed as astronauts. Until
they drown in our songs (which sounds poetic
but that's all an *aria* is—air, stupid).
Which is to say I'm angry we are
always drowning but we cannot drown
quick enough: our smoggy water, our
factory farmed air, my own airless poems.

Beauty can't be ethereal. I need
a heavyweight, an anchor, pocket-stones.
I am as old as Torricelli
was when he contracted typhoid;
if I drown, there'll be no monument
to all I have avoided.

PORTRAIT OF THE ARTIST AS
A BOG BODY

Bring a flaughter spade
        on our first date.
Search out my fingers
        under the turf's muck.
Stroke my hair, softer
        than the moss.

Come meet my friends sometime.
        I have thousands,
compressed under the sponge
        with their pretty cut throats.
We keep writing what we
        know—scapegoats and rope.

We keep waiting to be the
        next ones exposed and
hoisted up, rediscovered
        by anthology or
dismembered
        by backhoe.

SOURCES

portrait of the twentieth century as a plagiarist: a cento
Sources, in order of appearance: Alexander Graham Bell, Max Planck, T.S. Eliot, Edna St. Vincent Millay, Enrico Fermi, Hart Crane, John Ashbery, Albert Einstein, Niels Bohr, Adrienne Rich, Nirvana, Sylvia Plath.

portrait of the artist, gaslit
Borrows a line from a 2017 open letter from Amber Tamblyn to James Woods: "I see your gaslight & now will raise you a scorched earth." The "truffula tree" is borrowed from Dr. Seuss's *The Lorax.*

portrait of the artist reading the newspaper
Borrows a line from the band Fugazi's song "Merchandise": "You are not what you own."

portrait of the artist in the pediatrician's waiting room
"140 children" refers to the April 2018 discovery of a ritual mass child sacrifice in Peru.